Kids love reading
Choose Your Own Adventure®!

"When I figured out there were maps on the back, I almost exploded!"

Sophia DeSanto, age 9

"I read them because they are interesting, and they have lots of cool titles and words to use."

Laini Ribera, age 9

"There can be at least 28 ENDINGS in it and so many choices. Other books you have to read the whole book in order, well not this one!"

August Backman, age 10

"I like that you can choose. So, if you want to choose something, you can do it."

Colin Lawrence, age 10

"The CYOA books are crazy because there are so many crazy choices."

Isaiah Sparkes, age 12

RETURN OF THE NINJA

BY JAY LEIBOLD

ILLUSTRATED BY MICHAEL TONN
COVER ILLUSTRATED BY CHLOE NICLAS

CHOOSECO
WAITSFIELD, VERMONT

Book design: Stacey Boyd, Big Eyedea Visual Design

For information regarding permission, write to:

CHOOSECO

P.O. Box 46, Waitsfield, Vermont 05673
www.cyoa.com

Publisher's Cataloging-In-Publication Data
Names: Leibold, Jay, author. | Tonn, Michael, illustrator. | Niclas,
Chloe, illustrator.
Title: Return of the ninja / by Jay Leibold ; interior artwork: Michael
Tonn ; cover artwork: Chloe Niclas.
Other Titles: Choose your own adventure.
Description: [Revised edition]. | Waitsfield, Vermont : Chooseco,
[2019] | Originally published: New York : Bantam, ©1989. Choose your
own adventure ; 92. | Interest age level: 009-012. | Summary: "There is
something terribly wrong at your ninja friend Nada's magical dojo in
Japan. Nada believes there is an ancient curse so powerful that it is
killing her grandmother. YOU are a courageous and skilled ninja, but the
threats to Nada's dojo will take all of your skills. Will you be a match
for the shugenda warrior priests who hide in the rural mountainside? Keep
your friends close, and your shuriken closer"--Provided by publisher.
Identifiers: ISBN 1-937133-34-6 | ISBN 978-1-937133-34-4
Subjects: LCSH: Ninja--Japan--Juvenile fiction. | Grandmothers--Japan--
Juvenile fiction. | CYAC: Ninja--Japan--Juvenile fiction. | Grandmothers-
-Japan--Fiction. | LCGFT: Action and adventure fiction. | Choose-your-own
stories.
Classification: LCC PZ7.L53276 Re 2019 | DDC [Fic]--dc23

Published simultaneously in the United States and Canada

Printed in Canada

10 9 8 7 6 5 4 3 2 1

SPECIAL NOTE ON THE *NINJA*

According to legend, mountain creatures called *tengu* first taught the *ninja* their art. They also taught them *kuji* (sorcery) and how to use mystic finger positions to channel energy, key into the underlying forces of the universe, and alter the fabric of space and time.

Each *ryu* (tradition or school) has its own specializations and secrets, which are taught by a *sensei* (master or teacher) at the *dojo* (the place where martial arts are practiced). A student of *ninjutsu* will learn techniques of empty-handed combat, the use of weapons and special devices, as well as tactics of escape, deception, and invisibility, and the strategies of espionage, attack, and defense.

The ancient art of *ninjutsu* was developed in the eleventh and twelfth centuries by Japanese mountain clans. Drawing on their knowledge of martial arts, war tactics, and mystical practices—especially those in a branch of Buddhism known in Japan as *Shugendo*—they passed their art from one generation to the next.

In this book, YOU are a modern-day *ninja*. You are presented with a challenge on the very first day of teaching at Nada's *dojo*, but it is not the challenge you expected. You notice a figure on the roof of the *dojo* and quickly utilize your *ninjutsu* training to track down what you think you saw because, as a trained *ninja*, nothing should be ignored. Using bravery, *karate*, and specialized weapons, a *ninja* may succeed in their quest—but a *ninja* also knows when to ask for help. The adventures in this book include time travel, disguises, and weapons such as *shuriken, metsubishi*, and of course, the powerful sword of the Miyamotori family.

BEWARE and WARNING!

This book is different from other books.

You and YOU ALONE are in charge of what happens in this story.

There are dangers, choices, adventures, and consequences. YOU must use all of your numerous talents and much of your enormous intelligence. The wrong decision could end in disaster—even death. But don't despair. At any time, YOU can go back and make another choice, alter the path of your story and change its result.

You study *ninjutsu* at your friend Nada's dojo in the mountainous Nara region of Japan. Nada tells you her grandmother is suffering from a sudden and mysterious illness. She needs your help to take over teaching classes at the dojo so she can care for her grandmother. Your first day of teaching goes well until, suddenly, you notice a flash of movement on the roof. Your *ninja* training has taught you that even the smallest thing cannot be ignored. You decide to investigate, but you have a choice to make first. Do you organize the class to help search the house OR do you investigate on your own? The choice is yours. Good luck!

It is a sunny, quiet spring morning when your friend Nada receives a telephone call. After she ends the call, her face looks worried.

"My grandmother is very sick," she says. "It's a mysterious illness. No one can figure out what's causing it. I'm going to her house to see if I can help. Can you take charge of the *dojo* while I'm gone?"

You've been studying at Nada's *dojo* for a long time, but you're not sure if you're ready to teach the class.

"I'll do my best," you say. "I still have so much to learn myself."

"Don't worry," Nada says. "Just stick to the basics. The students need more of that anyway."

"Okay, I'll do it," you say.

"Good," Nada says. "I have to leave right away. My grandmother needs me."

Before Nada leaves, she tells you where her grandmother lives. "Her house is on a remote mountainside. There's no cell phone service, so I won't be able to call you. But I'll come back as soon as I can."

Nada's taxi arrives, and you wish her luck as she jumps in. "I'm sure everything will be fine," she calls out the window as the cab speeds away.

Turn to the next page.

2

Later, as you wait for the students to arrive, you think back on the events that brought you here to be a student and teacher at Nada Kurayama's family *dojo* in the mountainous Nara region of Japan.

A year has passed since you helped Nada solve the mystery of an ancient sword that had been sent to the *dojo*. The sword had terrible powers that nearly caused the destruction of the martial arts school. You and Nada discovered that, in the sixteenth century, the sword had belonged to a *ninja* named Sanchiro Miyamotori. He had used the sword to terrorize the countryside until, finally, he was killed by an ancestor of Nada's. Miyamotori died leaving a curse on the Kurayama family, and when the sword came to Nada's *dojo*, the *kami*, or spirit, of the *ninja* was stirred up. You and Nada had to use all your ingenuity and martial arts skills to figure out a way to placate the angry *kami*.

During this adventure, you found out that Nada's was a *ninja* family that went back hundreds of years. Nada explained that she had given up *ninjutsu*, but after your adventure, she began studying it again. Although you had originally come to Japan to study *aikido*, another form of martial arts, you decided to join Nada at her *dojo* and study *ninjutsu* as well.

Over the past year, you've been learning the many skills and techniques that are part of becoming a *ninja*. The first thing you learned from Nada is that *ninjutsu* is not like other martial arts.

Go on to the next page.

"I know this sounds complicated," Nada told you, "but *ninjutsu* is really a very practical art. Unlike the *samurai*, *ninja* do not worry about style, or honor, or glory. We start with very basic exercises in movement and meditation and make them part of our everyday lives. We want, after many years of study, to 'forget' our training and to achieve a state of complete emptiness that is also complete awareness and readiness."

You knew learning to become a *ninja* would be difficult, but you began working your way through the five stages of training, which correspond to the five elements—earth, water, fire, wind, and the Void. First you became familiar with your own physical capabilities and limits. Then you learned how to deal with an attacker, and how to enter the flow of conflict, seeing yourself and your enemy as inseparable parts of a whole. Finally, you attempted to put yourself in the center of danger without fear, where you could change the appearance of a situation so that what seemed to be weakness became strength. Along the way, you learned the *ninja* techniques of stealth and invisibility, including methods of escape, concealment, and disappearing. You practiced empty-hand combat and self-defense, methods of jumping and climbing, and the arts of spying and strategy.

You have yet to reach the final level, the Void, in which you leave behind your training. "Some day," Nada told you, "you will learn *mikkyo*, or esoteric knowledge. Esoteric knowledge is the highest knowledge of all."

Turn to the next page.

The students begin arriving for the first exercises of the day, and you join them in the courtyard, a little nervous about taking over as teacher.

Everything goes well until late in the morning. As you're leading the class through some training drills, you happen to glance up at the roof of the house. Something catches your eye. It's just a tiny bit of black movement, no more than a flicker. It could be a bird.

In the past, you might have paid no attention to such a small detail. But now, your *ninja* training has taught you that even the littlest thing cannot be ignored. You'll have to investigate, if only to find out you're getting too jumpy.

You begin to tell the class to carry on with their drills while you go inside. Then it occurs to you that you could have them help investigate as part of their training.

If you organize the class to help you search the house, turn to page 7.

If you think it's better not to involve the class, turn to page 10.

Clapping your hands to get the class's attention, you announce, "We're going to put some of our training to work. An intruder may have entered the house. We're going to make a thorough search of it."

You divide the class into groups, giving each group a part of the house to search. Taking four students with you, you circle around to the back of the house where you think you'd be most likely to catch an intruder.

Before you open the door, you ask the students which one of the five different ways of approaching danger you should take.

"The fire approach," a student named Basho says. "Let's set a trap."

"What do you think about the water approach?" you suggest. "That way we can dodge an attack."

"But it might let the intruder get away," Basho responds.

You wonder if you should let Basho have his way and take the more aggressive fire approach, rather than the defensive water approach.

If you accept Basho's suggestion to set up a trap, turn to the next page.

If you decide to take a defensive approach, turn to page 36.

8

"Okay," you say to Basho, "we'll take the fire approach. How do you plan to set your trap?"

"Wait here," Basho says. He runs off, then returns with a *kyoketsu shoge*, a rope with a steel ring at the end.

"You go in first," Basho tells you, "and draw the intruder out. We'll wait back here, and when he attacks you, we'll spring the trap on him."

You go along with Basho's plan, doubtful that it will work. You walk into the house, open and unguarded. To your surprise, you're immediately flattened by some immense force from above. You quickly realize the intruder is a *ninja*, an incredibly strong one, and he's got you pinned to the floor.

Basho and the other students burst in. Basho throws the ring, knocking the *ninja* on the head. The *ninja* grabs the ring, but the other students hold him back, and Basho wraps him up with the rope. This gives you a chance to apply a nerve pinch that leaves the *ninja* unconscious.

Now you've got a *ninja* on your hands, and you have no idea what to do with him. You have to act quickly because, once he comes to, you doubt you'll be able to keep him under control.

You wish Nada were here. But since her grandmother has no phone, the only way to reach her would be to go up to her grandmother's house, with the *ninja* in tow. It might be easier just to turn him over to the police.

If you call the police, go on to the next page.

If you want to go to Nada's grandmother's house, turn to page 24.

"Hello, police?" you say into your phone. "I've caught someone breaking into my house. Could you send an officer over right away?" Five minutes later, two police officers arrive. They see the *ninja* unconscious on the floor and eye you suspiciously.

You tell them the whole story, from when you saw movement on the roof to how your students helped capture the intruder. "I guess you have enough witnesses," one of the officers says. "But be sure you're available for questioning."

"I will," you promise as they load the unconscious body into their car.

The next day you read in the newspaper about a *ninja* escaping from the local jail.

Nada returns in the afternoon. After you've told her what happened while she was away, she says, "When I arrived at my grandmother's, I found out that she was sick because she was being slowly poisoned. It was a *ninja* poison. Once I figured that out, I knew what antidote to give her."

"So what probably happened was that the *ninja* poisoned your grandmother to draw you away from the *dojo*," you reason. "Then yesterday he broke in."

"I think you're right," Nada says. "But what's the purpose behind all of this?"

"I don't know," you say, "but I think we should be ready for the *ninja's* next move."

But his next move never comes. There's no sign of the *ninja* after that, and you're at a loss to explain the incident.

The End

10

You call the class to attention and say, "I must go into the house for a few moments. Continue with your exercises and wait for me to come back." You slip into the house, and employing *onshinjutsu*, you investigate every corner of the house—the basement, the roof, even the secret compartments and trapdoors. You find nothing, but you sense someone was there.

When you go back outside, several students run toward you, crying, "Come quick! Help!"

You race back to the training grounds. "Someone kidnapped Yoshi," a student says breathlessly. "We didn't notice until it was too late. A man just came out of the trees and grabbed him. We heard Yoshi cry out, and we ran after him, but they both disappeared."

"Can you describe the kidnapper?" you ask, trying to contain the panicky feeling spreading inside you.

"He was dressed in black," another student says. "I think he was a *ninja*."

Oh, no, you think. Your first day alone at the *dojo*, and one of the students is kidnapped by a *ninja*!

But there's no time for feeling sorry. You hesitate for a moment, trying to decide whether you should go inside and call the police, or whether you should chase after the kidnapper immediately.

If you ask the students which way the ninja *went, go on to the next page.*

If you decide to call the police, turn to page 14.

"Which way did they go?" you ask.

The students point you in the direction of the deep wooded hillside, and you take off. The *ninja* leaves very few signs of his flight, but you're still able to follow him using *ninja* tracking methods.

The tracks lead in an unexpected direction. They take you into the hills, higher and higher, toward the mountains to the east. You pursue the *ninja* relentlessly, up through forests and meadows, but still you don't catch sight of him or Yoshi.

The sun sinks toward the horizon. Your legs ache and your lungs burn. Coming up over the crest of a steep ridge, you suddenly stop dead in your tracks.

You're in a clearing. A broken-down building of some kind sits in the center. It looks like it may have been a lodging house at one time. Now it's overgrown with weeds and the windows are broken and burned out.

You scour the area around the clearing looking for signs of the *ninja*, but there are none. The vacant building appears to be the only place he could have gone.

Turn to the next page.

12

Silently you approach the building. Something at the entrance catches your eye: a piece of white cloth dangling on a nail. You realize it's a piece torn from Yoshi's robe!

You touch the cloth thoughtfully and continue into the house, your ears pricked for any sound. All you hear is the wind whistling through the windows. All you see is dust in the rays of the setting sun. Then you spot another bit of white cloth at the foot of a staircase. It's just like the piece you found on the nail. You look up the dark stairs, unable to see where they lead.

All of a sudden, you realize that the bits of cloth may have been a little too easy to find. Maybe the *ninja* wants you to come up the stairs—maybe he's waiting for you at the top. You wonder if you should go outside and see if there's another way to get up to the second floor.

On the other hand, you're receiving no sense of danger coming from the top of the stairs from your *sakki*, and you're reluctant to go back outside when you seem to be so close to finding Yoshi.

If you go up the stairs, turn to page 114.

If you go back outside, turn to page 121.

You run back into the house and call the police, asking them to block off all the roads in the area. The police tell you to get all the other students inside the *dojo* and stay there until they arrive.

You follow instructions and soon some officers arrive. A man in an overcoat walks over to you. "I'm Detective Jonsuro," the man says. "What happened?"

You go over every detail of the incident, and Jonsuro asks, "Do you have any idea who this *ninja* is? Why would someone want to kidnap Yoshi?"

"I don't know," you say.

Go on to the next page.

"We'll talk to Yoshi's family," the detective says. "Maybe the kidnapper wants ransom from them."

"I doubt it," you comment.

"Why?" the detective asks sharply.

"I'm not sure," you have to admit. "It's just a feeling."

"Well, stay at the *dojo* until we get back to you," he instructs.

"What about Nada?" you say.

"We'll speak with her right away," Jonsuro promises.

Once all the police officers leave, there's nothing for you to do but wait. You hear nothing for the rest of the day, but in the evening, Yoshi's father calls. "If you don't get Yoshi back safely, we'll see to it that your *dojo* is closed down," his father threatens.

"I'll do my best," you try to assure him. But you go to bed feeling very depressed.

Turn to the next page.

16

The next morning Nada and Detective Jonsuro both show up at the *dojo*. You tell Nada the whole story and then ask about her grandmother.

"She was sick from *ninja* poison," Nada explains. "I was able to counteract it. But I suspect the real purpose for the poisoning was to draw me away from the *dojo* so that the *ninja* could attack."

At that moment, your phone rings, a blocked caller. Detective Jonsuro waves for you to answer it.

"Hello?" you ask, trying to keep your voice normal.

A muffled voice says, "Do you want Yoshi back alive?"

"Yes, of course," you reply.

"Then give me the sword," the voice says.

"What sword?"

"You know what I'm talking about," the voice replies savagely. The call disconnects.

Nada and Jonsuro watch anxiously. "It was the kidnapper," you tell them. "He said he wants the sword."

"What sword?" Jonsuro asks.

"I wonder if he means the sword that was sent to the *dojo* last year," you muse.

"That must be it," Nada says. "We never did find out where the sword came from. Maybe it was stolen from him."

"Where's the sword now?" the detective asks.

Go on to the next page.

"The sword is gone," Nada answers. "And there's no way to get it back."

Before she can go on, the phone rings again. You answer as the other two watch.

The sound of Yoshi's voice tears at you. "Don't worry, I'm all right—" he says, before the muffled voice comes on the line and demands, "I want the sword—now!"

You wonder if you should buy time by telling the *ninja* he can have the sword. Or should you try to explain that the sword is gone forever?

If you say you'll give him the sword,
turn to the next page.

If you tell him the sword is gone,
turn to page 102.

"We'll give you the sword," you say quickly, "but it will take us a few days to get it. And when we give you the sword, you'll hand over Yoshi?"

"Correct," the kidnapper says.

"Where shall we make the exchange?"

"You will go to the mountain village of Kanayama," he instructs. "There is a telephone in the post office. It will ring at noon, three days from now. You will come absolutely alone. Believe me, I will know if you don't."

After you hang up, Nada blurts out, "Why did you do that? We don't have the sword!"

"I figured we could buy time by saying we'd give him the sword," you say. "At least now we know where he'll be in three days."

"Well," Jonsuro says, "I suppose that's better than nothing. But we don't have much to go on."

"Maybe we can make a copy of the sword," you suggest.

Nada shakes her head. "You remember that sword. It had great power. If the *ninja's* connected with it in any way, he'll recognize a fake immediately."

The detective leaves, saying he'll call you if he comes up with anything.

You manage to get a little rest, until your phone rings once again. Nada answers for you this time, and you watch her cringe as she listens. After she disconnects the call, she tells you, "That was Yoshi's parents again. Somehow they heard about the sword. They said if we don't turn it over to the *ninja*, they'll have us put in jail."

Go on to the next page.

The next morning things get worse. Headlines like NINJA KIDNAPPING are spread all over the newspapers.

Soon the phone is ringing off the hook, and reporters are buzzing the doorbell. They ask you to describe the kidnapping over and over again. They want to know every detail about the sword and your activities at the *dojo*. They even ask whether you're involved in a blood feud with another *ninja* clan. Afraid they'll find out you no longer have the sword, you and Nada tell the reporters as little as you can. When they ask if the kidnapper has called, you say, "No comment."

The stream of reporters, photographers, and television cameras seems to have no end. Everyone repeatedly asks you questions about how you feel. Finally, late in the afternoon, you get a moment alone with Nada in the kitchen. "I can't take much more of this," you say wearily.

"Well," Nada says thoughtfully, "we don't have to if we don't want to."

"They won't leave us alone just because we ask them to," you inform her.

"That's not what I meant," Nada replies. "This is our chance. We could slip into the secret passageways under the house and hide out until it's time to meet the kidnapper."

If you agree with Nada's suggestion to sneak away, turn to the next page.

If you think it's a bad idea to hide out, turn to page 109.

"Okay," you say to Nada, "let's get out of here. I'm sick of these reporters."

The two of you slip through a secret door in the hallway and follow a passage that goes under the *dojo* and comes out in the woods a kilometer away. You walk to the nearest road and catch a bus to a friend's house. There you try to call Detective Jonsuro to let him know what you're doing, but the lines to the police station are busy all day.

"Probably the reporters," Nada says. "We'll have to wait until tomorrow. Meanwhile, what are we going to do about Yoshi?"

You and Nada think and think, but you can't come up with any ideas on Yoshi's kidnapping or why the *ninja* wants the sword. You call the Miyamotori family, whose ancestor was the original owner of the sword, but they don't want to get involved.

You get through to Detective Jonsuro the next morning. "I haven't found any leads," he says. "What about you?"

"Nothing," you say.

"We'll keep trying," he says grimly. "Meanwhile, I'm going to have a copy of the sword made. Can you tell me what it looked like?"

You and Nada describe the sword for him, and promise you'll call back at the end of the day.

When you call again, you tell Jonsuro you don't know any more than you did that morning. "Neither do I," he confesses. "And we're out of time. Tomorrow is the day you're supposed to turn over the sword."

Go on to the next page.

"I guess we'll just have to hope the fake sword works," you say.

"I'm having a homing device built into it," he says. "That may be our best chance for getting Yoshi back alive."

The next morning you and Nada meet Jonsuro at the police station. A throng of reporters still buzzes around the station, waiting for news.

Turn to the next page.

As the detective drives you and Nada up to the village of Kanayama, you notice a car keeps reappearing behind you. "I think we're being followed," you say.

Detective Jonsuro screeches into a U-turn and guns the car up a side road. He races through a dizzying series of turns that eventually brings you back onto the main road. The maneuver seems to have taken care of the car that was following you.

Jonsuro stops just outside the town of Kanayama a few minutes before noon. Taking the sword out of the trunk, he points to a tiny jewel on the hilt. "There's a tracking device here," he says, handing the sword to you. "Good luck."

Alone, you walk through the village to the post office. You're startled to see the car that had been tailing you parked nearby. But you have no time to worry about it now.

Go on to the next page.

Exactly at noon, the telephone rings. You pick it up. "Go to the north end of the village. A path leads into the woods and up the mountain." *Click*.

You do as you're instructed. The path climbs steeply through the woods. Then, suddenly, you hear two cries from below. You run down the path. Turning a corner, you nearly trip over two people crumpled on the ground, victims of *ninja* daggers. And right in front of you are two *ninja*!

You recognize the victims as two of the reporters who have been following the kidnapping story—a little too closely, it seems.

Your first impulse is to run. But then you remember that you have the sword. Even though you haven't studied much *kendo*, or sword work, your skills might be good enough to hold them off.

If you draw the sword, turn to page 115.

If you think you'd better not, turn to page 90.

"How can we keep control of this *ninja* while I call a taxi to go to Nada's grandmother's house?" you wonder out loud.

"Let's put him in a trunk!" a student named Hisa suggests. The class helps you to tie up the *ninja* with boa knots, constrictor knots, and diamond knots, load him into a trunk, and lock it tightly. When the taxi arrives, you explain to the driver, "I need to get this trunk to my grandmother's house. It's a big fare. The house is three hours away. I'll pay you double what's on the meter—and a big tip."

This makes the driver happy. He helps you lash the trunk to the roof. You thank your students, and you're on your way.

Everything goes smoothly until you're on the final steep mountain grade to Nada's grandmother's house. The trunk begins shaking violently back and forth on the roof. The *ninja* has woken up and is trying to break out!

"What's going on here?" the driver demands. You try to act innocent. "What do you mean?" "That does it," the driver says. He pulls over to the side of the road and, leaving the engine running, jumps out to look at the trunk.

You eye the steering wheel. Should you jump into the front seat and drive away? You've had some driving lessons, and you figure if you drive fast enough you might make it to the house before the *ninja* breaks free. But you could also try to convince the taxi driver to keep going instead.

If you decide to drive yourself, turn to page 98.

If you try to talk to the driver, turn to page 103.

With your earplugs in, the *ninja* will not be able to trap you by deceiving your hearing. But you'll have to rely on your *sakki* to detect harmful intentions.

At first, you're disoriented because your ears aren't giving you clues. You realize you must allow yourself to be receptive to the anger of the intruder.

You move through the house with silent feet, using shadows and light for concealment. As you move, you feel something strange. You're picking up vibrations. The presence in the house is like a wind on your skin.

You keep moving, drifting just out of reach of the presence, yet staying close enough that you can still feel it. Though you've seen nothing yet, you can tell the presence is getting closer. You must move faster—it's coming in on you—now it's attacking!

Turn to the next page.

In a flash, you crouch and roll sideways, crashing into a ten-foot-tall wooden chest that stands upright against the wall. You must have hit the chest exactly right because a secret compartment large enough to walk through falls open. At the same moment, an object—probably a deadly *shuriken*—thunks high into the wood of the chest. You step inside the compartment and close yourself into the chest for protection.

Inside the chest, you open a second secret door that leads to a hidden passage behind the wall. For all the intruder can tell, you've just disappeared. You remove the earplugs, and through the wall, you hear a grunt of frustration.

You wait in tense silence for his next move. He leaves the room that the chest is in. You go down the hidden passage to a spot where you can hear anything in the house.

A few moments later, you hear sounds coming from one of the storerooms in the basement. You hurry down a passageway toward loud crashing sounds, as if the storeroom's being torn apart.

When you reach the basement, the storeroom is quiet. Cautiously you push open a secret panel that lets you out into the room. The contents of the room are strewn about in chaos. You rush out after the intruder, but already, you can sense that he has gone.

Turn to page 28.

28

You go back to the storeroom and try to put things in order. Nothing seems to be missing. He must not have found what he was after.

You're unsure what to do next. If you go to Nada's grandmother's house, you'll have to leave the *dojo* unguarded. You decide it can wait until morning.

Sleeping fitfully, as a part of you is on watch all night, you're woken by a knock on the door.

"I am Maki, Nada's grandmother," a small, steely-haired woman says. "We have problems."

"Come in, *Obasa*," you say.

You prepare some morning tea, but before you can tell Maki about last night, she launches into her own story. "A *ninja* came bursting into my house around midnight. He demanded we give him a sword. Of course, we didn't know what he was talking about. Then Nada realized he wanted the sword that was sent to the *dojo* last year—the one that caused you and her so much trouble."

"So that's what it was," you interrupt. "An intruder broke in here last night and made a mess of the storeroom. It must have been the *ninja*, looking for the sword. When he didn't find it, he went to your house. But—I thought you were sick."

"I was," she replies, "but Nada figured out that

Go on to the next page.

I was being poisoned. Not only that, it was a *ninja* poison. Luckily, she knew how to counteract it."

"So your poisoning was probably a ploy to draw Nada away from the *dojo*," you say.

"Without a doubt," Maki agrees.

Turn to the next page.

"Who is this *ninja*?" you ask.

"It was hard to tell, he was babbling so," Maki says. "But from what I could understand, his name is Hitari, and somehow he's related to the Miyamotori family. He kept talking about how the sword was his rightful inheritance, and he was going to avenge his family honor."

"What happened to his family honor?"

"It seems that a thousand years ago, his ancestor Mito Hitari was sent into exile for trying to kill his brother Taro. Mito's brother later started what became the Miyamotori branch of the family. Hitari claimed that his ancestor was wrongly exiled, and that by getting the sword, he would restore the Hitari family's rightful place."

"Did Nada tell him the sword is gone?"

"She certainly tried to." Maki sighs. "But he wouldn't believe her. He said she wanted to steal his powers, and she had the sword hidden somewhere."

"So—where are they now?"

"Well," Maki replies, "that's hard to say. Nada and Hitari became locked in a contest of wills. At the time, I wasn't yet strong enough to help Nada. The battle moved outside, into the woods, where, from what I could hear, it went on for most of the night."

Go on to the next page.

Maki pauses before continuing, "This may sound strange, but I know you will understand from your previous adventures with Nada. I believe the battle entered the time dimension. It became so intense that they broke out of this time and place and went back to a time a thousand years ago, when Hitari's ancestor lived."

"Then I must go back there and help Nada," you say.

"It is dangerous," Maki protests. "You do not know enough. If you don't find her, you may be stranded in the past."

"But I have to find Nada!"

"There are risks in either case," Maki says. "The choice is yours to make."

If you insist on going into the past to find Nada, turn to the next page.

If you agree with Maki that it's wiser not to travel through time, turn to page 58.

32

"I'm going after Nada," you say firmly. "I will brave the time travel. I can't abandon her."

"I can see you are determined," Maki says. "Well, perhaps you're right. The *ninja* Nada is battling is very powerful and full of anger. She'll need all the help she can get. I can help you go into the past. But we should not waste any time. You must get ready immediately."

You spend the rest of the day preparing to go back to the tenth century. There's a lot to learn about the customs and habits of the era, which are very different from the present.

At a time when Europe was in chaos and the Americas were still untouched by the sword of conquest, Japan enjoyed a flowering of its civilization in peace and tranquility. The country was ruled by a tiny minority of the population, the Heian aristocracy. Most of them lived in the beautiful capital city of Kyoto.

The values of the era were very different from those of the violent centuries that were to follow. Delicacy of feeling and poetic expression were considered the marks of the "good persons." The aristocracy looked down upon those who were militaristic, or who came from the provinces, or who did manual labor. There was no need for the *samurai* and their code of honor. Nor was *ninjutsu* known, except perhaps among a few mountain monks defending themselves against religious persecution.

Turn to page 34.

34

As Maki watches you finish your preparations, she reminds you that you have an important decision to make.

"Before you go into the past, you must choose how you will disguise yourself," she says. "I suggest you dress as a Buddhist monk."

"Why not as a carpenter?" you ask. "When Nada and I went into the past before, we disguised ourselves as carpenters."

"You must remember that the aristocracy of the tenth century had no respect for working people. In the minds of the nobles, there was doubt as to whether common people were even human—and the nobles treated them as if they were not. The aristocracy would think nothing of abusing, enslaving, or even killing a laborer. But as a monk, you would be treated with some respect."

"That's true," you reply. "And no one would question my right to travel. But suppose I have to demonstrate my religious knowledge? If I disguise myself as a carpenter, I won't have to worry about that. Besides, I can always change my disguise."

"Either way will be a challenge," Maki says. "The choice is again yours to make."

If you decide to time travel dressed as a carpenter, go on to the next page.

If you choose the monk disguise, turn to page 44.

Once you've put together everything you'll need to appear as a tenth-century carpenter, Maki sits down with you. Using *saiminjutsu*, she puts you into a trance and then begins the *kuji* hand signs that will part the weave of time for you.

When you open your eyes, you're on a mountainside. A noise is coming down the mountain toward you. You scramble out of the way just as a mass of robed monks, carrying torches and all kinds of weapons, rumbles by, chanting angrily. You realize they're probably *shugenja*, or warrior priests, on a raid.

You wait until the way is clear to venture out and follow the path down the mountain through a moonlit forest. As you near the bottom, a view of a beautiful city opens before you. It is Kyoto.

The city is surrounded by a wall, and there are eighteen gates. You wonder if you'll be able to get through a gate at this time of night. You could wait until morning, when the gatekeepers will be less suspicious. Or, you could try to get into the city tonight by scaling the wall.

*If you try to scale the wall now,
turn to page 74.*

*If you decide it's better to go through a gate in
the morning, turn to page 84.*

36

"I think we'd better be more defensive," you say to Basho. "Let's use the water approach to search the house."

One by one, you and the four students slip into the house, moving with stealth, always listening for sounds that might give an intruder away. A slow and thorough search of the house reveals nothing. Still, you can't shake the feeling that someone has been there.

Back in the courtyard of the *dojo*, the other groups of students report that they found nothing either. Deciding there isn't anything else you can do, you resume the training drills.

Go on to the next page.

For the rest of the day, you're occupied with your classes. By the time you send the students home, you're tired from the long day of teaching.

Alone in the house, you begin to prepare your dinner. Thinking back on the flicker of movement you thought you saw, you wonder if maybe you were just nervous about being in charge of the *dojo* for the first time. You decide to forget about the incident.

As darkness falls, you begin to feel the emptiness of the house. Every little sound seems magnified. You can't help feeling that there's something odd about the silence.

Then, just as you finish eating, you hear a small but distinct sound from the other side of the house. For a moment, you want only to run away. Then you remind yourself that you're responsible for the safety of the *dojo*, and that you're also a *ninja* in training—it's time to use your knowledge.

Turn to the next page.

38

Though it seems odd, you realize that the first thing you must do is meditate in order to clear your mind for whatever is ahead. So, in spite of your racing adrenaline, you sit cross-legged, close your eyes, and begin breathing slowly.

As you enter a state of deeper listening, you're immediately aware that there is a presence in the house, and it's no ordinary intruder. It's a very strong presence, perhaps even a *ninja*.

Just then, a sound comes from the opposite side of the house. Then another from the roof.

Your eyes pop open. It's time to act—but where should you begin? You wonder if there is more than one person. You also remember that *ninja* can use sound vibrations to fool their victims. The noises might be traps set for you. You wonder if you'd be better off not to count on your sense of hearing. Maybe you should even cut off your hearing altogether, by using earplugs. That way you can focus on your *sakki*—a sixth sense used to detect harmful intentions.

If you decide to use earplugs and tune in to your sixth sense, turn to page 25.

If you decide not to use earplugs and instead use all of your senses, turn to page 123.

You start your attack by throwing a handful of *metsubishi*, or blinding powder, into the eyes of the officer nearest you. Then, grabbing the staff of one of your fellow prisoners, you use it as a *ninja hanbo* to knock down the next two officers who come at you, one with each end of the staff.

Now the other *shugenja* join in the fray, and there is confusion. An officer grabs your *hanbo* from behind. You twist under him and use the *hanbo* to flip him over your back. This gives you an opening to escape, and you take off down the side street.

To your surprise, the rest of the *shugenja* follow once they get free of the officers. All of you run until you think you've put enough distance between yourselves and the police.

"*Sensei*," one of the monks says to you, using a term of respect, "if not for you, we would surely have ended up in the emperor's dungeon."

You're taken aback at being called a *sensei*—but then you realize that the monks have probably never seen anything like what you just did. "I was just trying to help," you say modestly.

"You must come back to our monastery with us," another monk says. "We will show you our hospitality and properly express our gratitude. Perhaps you can tell us how you gained your powers." The others in the circle nod in agreement.

It's a delicate situation. You may give grave offense by refusing their offer. Besides, they may be able to help you. And if you stay in Kyoto, you risk capture by the police.

Turn to the next page.

42

You hike back up the mountain, surrounded by your new devotees. They're full of questions about your clothing and your accent. You answer them as best you can, saying you're from a far away province in Hokkaido. You hope no one is familiar with the region. Most of the *shugenja* seem happy to believe whatever you say.

"But, *sensei*," one of the monks says impatiently, "what we really want to know is how you learned your powers. Will you teach us?"

You ponder for a moment. The simplest thing to do might be to tell them about the art of *ninjutsu*, pretending that it has been developed by the monks in your province. It would create goodwill among the *shugenja* and convince them of your importance. Perhaps then they would help you find Nada.

But you also wonder if it's right to introduce these new ideas before their time. You could claim you're pledged to secrecy, refuse to talk, and hope they'll still be willing to help you find Nada.

If you decide to tell the shugenja *about* ninjutsu,
turn to page 70.

If you say you can't teach them,
turn to page 92.

44

Late in the evening, you are prepared to leave and travel through time, disguised as a monk. You sit down with Maki. She directs you in a series of meditations, focusing in on Nada and where in the weave of history she is. Maki intones the syllables of *kuji*, whose vibrations open the fabric of time. You fall into a trance as Maki puts you under the spell of *saiminjutsu*.

When you return to consciousness, different sensations hit you at once. You're standing on a steep mountainside. The rumble of feet and a frightening, relentless chant is coming from higher above you. When you look up, the glare of rushing torches hurts your eyes. A group of men dressed in clothes similar to yours are traversing a mountain path, and they appear armed and agitated.

Go on to the next page.

You think it's strange that Buddhist priests are carrying all sorts of weapons. But when you see their long hair, you realize that these are not just priests, they're *shugenja*, or mountain warrior priests, precursors of the *ninja*.

You blend in as you're swept up in the crowd. The horde of priests rumbles down the narrow mountain path. Soon a city appears below. When you get a glimpse of the magnificent buildings, you realize it's Kyoto. The priests must be on some sort of a raid. You don't want to give yourself away, so you just go along with them.

Turn to the next page.

46

The stampede barges past the terrified guards at one of the gates of the city and continues up a wide avenue. You're surprised to find that you're headed for the northern part of the city, where the imperial palace and government offices are. You begin to wonder what you've gotten yourself into.

Turn to the next page.

48

The march of warrior priests finally comes to a halt in front of the famous Bureau of Divination, also known as the Yin-Yang Bureau. There, the throng begins to yell angry demands, threatening to attack. From what you can hear, they want freedom to practice their religion without persecution from the government. You recall that at this time, *Shugendo* was a newly evolving set of beliefs that was viewed with suspicion by traditional Buddhists.

Soon a regiment of imperial police appears and cordons off the Yin-Yang building. You edge toward the back of the crowd.

Just as you reach the back of the throng, a gang of imperial police officers appears out of nowhere and surrounds a small group of protesters—including you. Before you know what's happening, the police herd the group into a side street, cutting you off from the rest of the *shugenja*.

"Come quietly, and no one will get hurt," a captain barks at you, his sword raised.

There's no way your group can overpower the police—unless you use *ninjutsu*. You suspect they've never seen it before, and the element of surprise might give you and the other *shugenja* a chance to break the cordon and escape.

On the other hand, if your plan doesn't work, you could be in worse trouble than you already are. You also wonder if it's wise to reveal the existence of such techniques before their time.

If you attack the police, using a ninja *move, turn to page 41.*

If you go quietly, turn to page 54.

"How do I find Sakai?" you ask the *shugenja*.

"Go up the road and take the right fork around to the other side of the mountain. After you cross the waterfall, there will be a small trail leading up the valley. Follow it, and where it bends to the right, you will see Sakai's hut."

You gather up your *furoshiki*, and set off up the road. You travel through the night. Finally, at daybreak, you find the track up to Sakai's house. You find Sakai, a small, somber man, engrossed in his morning rituals. You introduce yourself, and explain who sent you. "I understand you are in the service of Mito Hitari," you say.

Sakai looks suspicious, so you explain, "I'm looking for a friend who I think may be in danger."

Sakai looks you over, then invites you into his hut. Once you convince him you're not a friend of the Hitari, he begins to talk.

"Mito Hitari enlisted me to help him. He told me that his brother Taro had betrayed him. I performed many kinds of sorcery against Taro, but none of them worked. It is because Mito's intentions are bad. He is envious of his brother."

"Have you told him this?" you ask.

"It would be the end of me. He is too powerful. Taro can't help me either—he would have me imprisoned for practicing sorcery against him. Who is your friend?"

"Her name is Nada," you say. "I think she's engaged in a fight with one of the Hitari."

Turn to the next page.

50

"I can take you to Mito's house," Sakai offers. "I will say you are my student. No one will suspect you are looking for Nada."

Sakai leads you on a secret path down the mountain and into the city of Kyoto. It takes most of the day to get to the Hitari house, but finally the two of you arrive at the front door. Sakai is greeted by the *rojo*, or house mistress.

"This is my disciple," Sakai tells her, introducing you. "There is no need to tell the master I am here, yet. I must attend to other business first."

The *rojo* bows and lets you in. You follow Sakai into the mansion, until finally he says, "Wait here. I will make some inquiries."

Half an hour later Sakai returns. "There is talk of a prisoner in the cellar," he whispers. "No one knows who it is or why the prisoner is there. They say a distant Hitari cousin just arrived from the provinces, and he is responsible for the prisoner. There were sounds of a fight last night."

Go on to the next page.

"Can we find the prisoner?"

Sakai checks to make sure no one is around. "Perhaps," he says. "Follow me."

You sneak through a small door that leads to a narrow set of stone steps. The steps descend into a complex of dank cellars. In one of the cellars, you find an unconscious figure curled up in a corner.

Turning the figure over, you barely recognize Nada. Her face is swollen and bruised. She slowly opens her eyes as you shake her. You can't tell if she recognizes you. You untie the ropes around her wrists and ankles and help her to her feet. "How do we get out of here?" you ask Sakai.

"The same way we came in," he replies. "But you are on your own now. I cannot risk being caught with you if you help her escape."

Turn to page 53.

You thank Sakai, and help Nada hobble toward the stairs. At last you reach the door and take Nada out to the garden, where you find a secluded spot to rest. Nada starts to return to her usual self. "Are you ready to return to the present?" you ask.

Somehow Nada finds the strength to put you into a trance and take both of you back to the *dojo*.

A couple of days later, while Nada is at her grandmother's being nursed back to health, she tells you what happened. "When the *ninja* and I went into the past, we discovered that his story was at least partly accurate. Mito Hitari was to be exiled for plotting to assassinate his brother Taro."

You then tell Nada how you met Sakai, after achieving fame as a teacher of *ninjutsu*, and how he confirmed that Mito's intentions were evil. "According to Sakai, Mito was simply envious of his brother."

"Well," Nada goes on, "instead of accepting this, the *ninja* became more enraged, and he took it out on me. I had no choice but to fight him in the garden. I felt I would lose, and I was right. That's the last thing I remembered until you came and rescued me."

"You did well," Nada's grandmother says to you. "But you also made a grave mistake. You should not have introduced ideas such as *ninjutsu* before their time. We can only hope that what you taught will fade out among the *shugenja* before any damage is done."

You will never know if your decision changed the course of history.

The End

54

You put up no resistance, and the police take you and the *shugenja* to the imperial prison. They put each of you into a separate cell, where you spend the rest of the night. You don't want to call attention to yourself, so you ask no questions.

In the morning, your hands are bound and you're taken to the Yin-Yang Bureau. You're set before a Buddhist priest, who looks down sternly at you.

"You were caught disturbing the peace and violating the sacred grounds of the Bureau of Divination. What is the purpose of this outrage?"

"I don't know," you say innocently. "I just arrived from a remote province in Hokkaido. I am a pilgrim. I know little of these matters. I came here to learn—"

"And what are your religious practices in Hokkaido?"

You know you can't show any hesitation. You blurt out some *ninja* philosophy, knowing it will sound strange to him.

The priest regards you for several minutes with expressionless eyes. Finally, he says, "It may be that you are telling the truth. You have a very strange way of speaking, and your philosophy is unfamiliar to me. Indeed, everything about you is peculiar. Nevertheless, you have committed a grave offense. I will have to speak to the emperor about you."

With that, you're dismissed and returned to your cell.

Turn to page 56.

56

The next morning, the priest shows up at your cell. "The emperor is curious," he says simply. "He will see you now."

You're escorted to the imperial palace. You're surprised at the simplicity of the grounds and of the emperor's residence, which is located in the innermost part of the Nine-Fold Enclosure. Pausing before the doors to the emperor's chamber, the priest murmurs, "Your fate will be determined by the impression you make upon the emperor." With that, he turns and leaves.

The emperor's chamber also seems unassuming. There is little color or ornamentation, and the only furniture is a small chair in which the emperor is seated. He is young, close to your age, with a smooth, fresh face. His features are fine, and there's a delicacy and grace about the way he moves.

You make your bow of homage, a slow, formal bow as far down as you can go. The emperor motions the guards to unbind your hands and leave the room.

"So," he says in a soft voice, "tell me about yourself."

Go on to the next page.

"Your Excellency," you stutter, "I come from a place far, far away, high in the mountains, whose cold and snow are far from civilization. I have come to your great city seeking wisdom."

A smile plays on his lips. "Tell me," he says, "do all the people from your region speak and act as strangely as you?"

"More or less," you reply uncertainly.

He seems amused by this. "More or less!" he says, clapping his hands. "What a charming answer."

You smile, unsure what he finds so charming. The subtle scent of his perfume wafts over you.

"Now," he says, smoothing his robes, "I understand you have some very unusual beliefs. Give me a demonstration. Show me an example of your art."

You wonder how to impress the emperor. Should you show him a series of *ninja* moves, maybe a back flip and succession of kicks, punches, and handsprings? He's probably never seen anything like that. Or should you try instead to make up some lines of *ninja* philosophy about the poetry inherent in movement?

The emperor waits expectantly.

If you attempt to do the ninja *moves, turn to page 64.*

If you try to recite the poetry, turn to page 66.

58

"I guess you're right," you say to Maki. "It's too dangerous to go into the past. What can we do instead?"

Maki rubs her chin. "Well...we can meditate and send out *kuji* to Nada, to make her stronger. And we can be prepared to help her when she and the *ninja* return."

For the next three days, you and Maki keep a vigil, hoping your meditations and *kuji* reach Nada. The hours stretch on endlessly as you wait for something to happen. Nothing does.

Then, on the fourth morning, Maki comes in and wakes you up before dawn. Her face is sad. "I had a dream," she says. "I'm afraid Nada won't be coming back."

You put your face in your hands. "I should have gone to help her."

"It is not your fault," Maki says gently. "Better that one of you, at least, is still here to run the *dojo*."

The End

"That's not important—do you want to meet with me or not?" you ask the *ninja*.

"I'll meet you," the *ninja* says. "But if you try anything, Yoshi will suffer for it."

"It's a deal," you say. "Where do we meet?"

"Go to the village of Kanayama. There is a public phone at the post office. It will ring at three o'clock this afternoon."

"I'll be there," you promise, and end the call.

"This is foolish," Detective Jonsuro starts, but you interrupt him.

"I think I can convince the *ninja* that we don't have the sword," you say. "I began to hear some doubt in his voice."

"We don't have much time to get to Kanayama," Nada says. "Let's go."

"I guess I can't stop you," the detective says with resignation, "so I'll give you a ride."

Jonsuro speeds up to Kanayama. You have him let you out short of the village so you can walk into the post office alone. Precisely at three the phone rings.

"Walk directly north out of the post office," a voice says. "You will find a path leading up the mountain ridge. Follow it."

Turn to the next page.

60

You follow the instructions, hiking up the steep path through a dense forest. The trail takes you higher and higher, until, two hours later, you turn a corner and suddenly come upon a small temple in a clearing. Just as suddenly, you're surrounded by three black-clad *ninja*.

The *ninja* escort you into the temple, where a small, somber man is seated on a pillow. He motions for you to sit down. The *ninja* leave.

"You were wise to come alone," he comments. "Now, tell me what you say has become of my sword."

You tell him the whole story, finishing with the discovery that the sword had inflamed the vengeful *kami* of Sanchiro Miyamotori, which tried to destroy the *dojo*.

"The most obvious solution," you conclude, "was for us to placate the *kami* and get rid of the sword."

Turn to page 62.

The *ninja* sits for a long while, saying nothing. You realize that he's meditating on what you've said. Finally, he speaks. "I must admit that your story has the ring of truth. I must also admit that I have learned from it. It may be that I, too, have been under the influence of a vengeful *kami*.

"You see," he explains, "My family, the Hitari, is a branch of the Miyamotori. A long time ago— exactly one thousand years ago, in fact—my ancestor was unjustly sent into exile. He was the victim of the scheming of his brother, who had been promoted to a high rank and did not want my ancestor as a rival. Sanchiro Miyamotori was the descendant of that scheming brother.

"Through all these centuries, our branch of the family has suffered in isolation. When I heard about the sword, I became convinced that if I could get it, I could redeem our lost honor. The sword and its power would be the foundation for my *ryu*. Through the *ryu*, my branch of the family would regain its prominence.

"Unfortunately, my brother got hold of the sword before I could. He sent it to your *dojo*, not only to spite me, but also to cause the destruction of your *dojo*. From what you say, his plan nearly worked.

"Now I can see that I've been in the grip of the angry *kami* of my ancestor. We two brothers have been repeating the mistake of our ancestors. Perhaps it is better, after all, that the sword is gone forever."

Go on to the next page.

The *ninja* stands up and shakes your hand. "Yoshi will be waiting for you at the post office," he says. "You will understand if I don't stay here any longer."

He turns and leaves, and you run back down the mountain path. Yoshi is waiting at the post office, as promised, and you take him back to Jonsuro and Nada for a happy reunion.

The End

64

You move into the middle of the room to leave more space for your *ninja* demonstration. You take deep breaths and flex your knees before you begin. The attendants stand back. With a shout, you do a back flip, and then a blinding series of punches and strikes, ending with a triple backward handspring.

Panting, you bow to the emperor after your performance. His face looks stricken. The attendants shrink away from you. You look at the emperor, waiting for his reaction.

"Yes," he finally manages to say in a restrained voice, "that was highly unusual." He motions quickly for you to be taken from the room.

The guards lead you back to your cell. A short while later, the priest comes to fetch you. "We are moving you to the Divination Bureau, where we can keep an eye on you," he says. "The emperor was quite horrified by your demonstration. He said he has never seen anything so vulgar and violent. He thinks you must be a very dangerous person, and he is concerned that this art not be spread throughout the country."

You're taken to the Yin-Yang Bureau under heavy guard. As they lock you up, you reflect dejectedly on how difficult it will be to escape.

The End

You don't have long to come up with some lines of poetry. The ability to recite quickly is considered a mark of a "good person."

"To forget your intention," you recite, "and let it flow together with thought and action, is to achieve the highest state of unthinking."

The emperor says nothing, and you wonder if you should go on. But then he comments, "I have never heard such ideas before. And you went right to the essence of the matter. Very thought-provoking."

He does seem lost in thought for a while, before he says, "Tell me more."

You begin to expound on your philosophy, starting slowly. But as the emperor repeatedly says, "Very interesting," you gain confidence and speak more freely.

Go on to the next page.

Finally, after two hours, the emperor grows tired. "This has been most intriguing," he says. "You please me. You must tell me if there is anything we can do to make your visit more pleasant."

"Actually," you speak up boldly, "there is. I came to Kyoto with a friend, but we've been separated. She is named Nada. In fact, she is my teacher."

"Hmm," the emperor muses, "I do believe there was a recent report of a visitor of that description. At the Hitari house, as I recall."

Your heart jumps when you hear this. The emperor calls an attendant to his side and begins giving instructions. You are led from the chamber, your audience with the emperor at a close.

Turn to the next page.

68

You're taken to a small room in the palace, where an attendant tells you to wait.

You sit on the floor. Every once in a while, you're brought tea and food. The hours drag by. Finally, you hear voices approaching. An attendant announces that you have a visitor.

"Nada!" you cry.

She rushes to greet you. "What are you doing here?"

Go on to the next page.

"Can't you see that I'm a guest of the emperor?" you exclaim. Once the attendant has left, you explain how you came into the past to help her.

"Well," Nada says, "you arrived just in time. The emperor's men just barely saved me from a fight with Hitari—a fight I think I would have lost."

"So what was all this about?"

"Hitari wanted the sword," Nada answers. "He thought he could use it to start a *ninja ryu*. This would help him restore the honor his family lost when his ancestor Mito was exiled in this time. But when Hitari and I got here, we saw that Mito truly did deserve his punishment—he was jealous of his brother and was plotting to kill him."

"Then why were you and Hitari about to fight?"

"Hitari couldn't accept the truth when he saw it. He turned his anger on me. But this is the nature of jealousy. He was infected by the spirit of his ancestor."

"Well, before he comes after us again," you say, "let's get out of here and get back to the present as fast as we can."

The End

70

You launch into a lecture on the art of *ninjutsu*. Your audience listens with rapt attention. Even after you reach the mountain monastery, they keep you talking late into the night.

Word of your exploits and teachings spreads quickly. You gain instant fame among the mountain *shugenja*. All through the next day, monks arrive to hear you speak. You're flooded with students, so many that it is impossible to escape them. You're a prisoner of your own success.

Finally, at the evening meal, exhausted from answering questions all day, you ask for something in return. "I need some help," you say. "I traveled here with my teacher. But we've been separated, and I must find her. She may be at the Hitari house."

One of the *shugenja* hesitates before asking, "Which Hitari?"

"I believe his name is Mito," you reply.

"Mito is feuding with his brother Taro," the *shugenja* explains. "It all started when Taro was raised to the third rank, while Mito remained on the fourth. He is jealous of his brother." The *shugenja* confers with his friends before going on. "We know a monk named Sakai who has been enlisted by Mito to help him overthrow his brother."

"Could I speak to Sakai?" you ask.

Go on to the next page.

"Of course," the *shugenja* replies. "He lives on the other side of the mountain. I will send for him." Just then a breathless messenger arrives from the city. "The Yin-Yang Bureau has heard about the new teacher. A regiment of imperial guards is on its way to arrest us all!"

"You must go," the *shugenja* tells you. "You can find Sakai's hut by yourself."

"No," you say, "I will stay and help you."

"You have helped us enough," he says. "You must look for your friend."

Maybe the *shugenja* is right—maybe you should go find Sakai. But he lives on the other side of the mountain, farther away from Kyoto. Besides, the monks may need you here.

If you try to find Sakai, turn to page 49.

If you stay with the shugenja, *turn to page 119.*

72

You jump off the wall into the Hitari garden and wait for dawn to come. There you change into clothes that will allow you to pass as a house servant and slip into the house through a side window.

For a while, you prowl through the house, listening, but you don't hear much. A few members of the staff give you questioning looks, but you just hurry by. Finally, your sharp ears pick up voices coming from a few rooms away. You glide silently among the screens that serve as walls in the house, until you can hear every word that is being said from behind one of them.

"But you can't just kill him!" a man is saying. "Everyone would know you ordered it. Besides, it would be very difficult."

"I must," another man says in a low voice full of anger. "For too long my brother has acted superior to me. For him to be promoted to the third rank, while I stay at the fourth, is the final outrage."

"Beg pardon, Lord Mito," the first man says soothingly, "but perhaps we should give our *shugenja*'s sorcery a chance to work." (You know that a *shugenja* is a religious sorceror.)

"He's had his chance," Mito says.

"But we must at least wait for some pretext for action—" the other pleads.

"I need no pretext!" Mito hisses. "I shall do as I want."

Just then, you hear movement from somewhere nearby. Mito hears it too. "What's that?" he says.

"I'll look," the other man says.

Go on to the next page.

Slipping away before Mito and his advisor catch you, you hurry to the back of the house. You pass through a sliding door into the garden and stop to think for a moment. From what you've overheard, Mito is plotting to kill his brother, which must be the reason he will eventually be exiled.

As soon as you turn the corner around a hedge into a small clearing by a pond, you see them— Nada and the *ninja* faced off against each other. Nada sees you immediately, and gestures to the *ninja* to wait, saying, "It's one of the servants." The *ninja* turns and waits for you to approach, keeping his eye on Nada at the same time. You play your part. "Pardon me," you say meekly, drawing close to the *ninja*, "but Lord Mito—" Before you finish your sentence, your arm strikes out, smashing the *ninja* on the neck. He crumples to the ground.

"Am I glad you came along," Nada says with a sigh of relief. "He insisted on fighting. I don't think I could have handled him alone."

You tell Nada what you just overheard in the house. "We were eavesdropping on the conversation too," she says. "But instead of convincing Hitari that his ancestor would be sent into exile for good reasons, it only made him angrier, and he insisted we fight it out."

You look down at Hitari. "What should we do about him?"

"He'll be taken care of by Lord Mito," Nada replies, "Let's leave him here and get back to our own time before anyone else comes out."

The End

74

You spot a good place to scale the wall. When you get up close, you see it is only about six feet high. You stand back, get a good run at it, and use your momentum to power up the wall and grab the top. You drop down on the other side and you're in the city.

From the look of the crumbling buildings and empty fields, you think you must be in the western part of Kyoto, which has seen many fires and has become more and more deserted over the years.

You wander through the eerily empty streets. A man stealing down a side street catches your eye. Cutting through an abandoned house, you intercept him at the next corner.

"Where is the Hitari house?" you blurt from a recess of the abandoned house.

The man jumps back when he hears your voice. "Did you say Hitari?"

"Yes, I'm looking for the residence of Mito Hitari."

He looks nervously at you. "Ah, I don't believe I know it," he says, and runs off.

There's something strange about the way he answered you. Thinking he may know more than he claims, you decide to follow him.

Using *ninja* techniques of stealth, you shadow the man through the streets of Kyoto. He never knows you are there.

Go on to the next page.

You follow the man into the wealthy eastern section of the city. He goes around to the back of one of these houses and slips through a hedge into a large garden. You see that he's headed for a lighted window at the back of the house.

You race around the other side of some bushes and cut him off before he reaches the window.

"I won't hurt you," you say, stepping up to him in a slightly threatening way. "Just tell me where the Hitari house is."

He nods over to your left. "It's on the other side of that wall. But please," he says, grabbing your sleeve, "don't tell them you saw me here."

Hoping he has information, you demand, "Why not?"

"A Hitari woman I know lives there," he says shyly, "and I am in love with her. But since I am below her station, they will kill me if they find out I am seeing her."

"Don't worry," you assure him, and disappear into the garden. You find the wall and use your *kaginawa* to climb it.

From the top of the wall, you eye the dark, massive Hitari house and think about how to get in. Should you sneak in wearing dark *ninja* clothes right now? Or should you wait until morning to disguise yourself as a servant, so that you can move freely through the house?

If you decide to wait until morning, turn to page 72.

If you decide to enter the Hitari house now, dressed as a ninja, *turn to page 78.*

You wrap a length of rope you still have in your pocket around the trunk of a tree, then lean out and use the rope to brace yourself while you walk, foot over foot, up the tree.

For a while, everything is silent. You wait, knowing that patience is the best—and only—strategy you have.

Suddenly, you hear Nada calling to you from the house, but you can't make out what she's saying. You don't want to give away your position by answering, but then you remember a trick you learned from her. You call back, but project your voice so that it sounds as if it's coming from the edge of the rock face.

Still you wait. You think Nada and the *ninja* must both be moving toward that spot, but neither makes a sound.

Then you see the *ninja*—below you, right at the edge of the rocks. You plan your leap carefully. You jump from the high tree into a smaller sapling that's between you and the *ninja*. The sapling bends with your weight, nearly to the ground, close enough to where you can hit the *ninja* squarely with a double-footed kick.

He never sees the blow coming. The kick knocks him to the edge of the rocks, where he desperately claws for a hold. He doesn't find one. With a scream he tumbles down the rock face.

Nada arrives a moment later. You both look over the edge of the rocks. There's no sign of life. "That must be the end of him," Nada says. "It's too bad we'll never find out what this was all about."

Go on to the next page.

Nada helps you back to the house. Your body hurts everywhere. Nada dresses your old wounds again, plus the new ones. "That will have to do for tonight," she says. "Try to get some sleep. I'll go for help in the morning."

You close your eyes as Nada stands up to turn off the light. Suddenly the sound of the window smashing jolts your eyes open. The *ninja* stands before you, bloodier than ever, with a crazed look in his eyes. Nada is on the floor next to the window.

You're too stunned to move. As the *ninja* raises a knife to throw at you, you feel you can only accept the end.

Then the *ninja* just crumples to the ground. Behind him you see Nada's grandmother, applying the death grip to his neck. She looks almost as dazed as you do, but, looking down at the *ninja*, she manages to explain, "I had no choice. Even before he returned, I'd woken up and I could feel his rage. My *sakki* told me it was the same rage that had tried to poison me. It was so powerful, I could do nothing else."

You nod in agreement, and lead Nada's grandmother back to her room.

The End

78

Still perched on the top of the wall, you dig through your *furoshiki* and quickly change into black *ninja* clothes that will help you to blend in with the shadows. You climb a tree that enables you to reach a gable of the house. Swinging hand over hand on the gable, you get your foot onto a window ledge and pull yourself in.

Staying low and using the shadows, you steal through the rooms, stopping in each to listen. Still you hear nothing—so you're stunned when you turn a corner and knock heads with another *ninja*!

He immediately attacks, grabbing your neck to pinch the vital nerve that will leave you unconscious. But someone approaches from behind and kicks the *ninja's* feet out from under him. The *ninja* falls to the floor, dragging you with him. You roll out of his grip as he uses his elbows to knock whoever is behind him so hard that the person crashes through a screen. That gives you the chance to grab the *ninja's* arm and throw him to the ground, but he uses his momentum to pull you along and flings you into another screen. You hear wood splintering.

As you clear your head, the *ninja* comes at you again. But suddenly, the other person comes flying out of nowhere—and now you see that it's Nada! She knocks the *ninja* down, but he gets her in an arm lock. You draw out your *kaginawa* and wrap it under the *ninja's* arms and over the back of his neck. This frees Nada, who helps you use the cord of the *kaginawa* to tie him up.

Meanwhile, you hear shouts throughout the house, and footsteps coming your way.

Turn to page 80.

80

"There they are!" someone cries. You and Nada heave the *ninja* down the corridor and into the path of five of the household staff coming at you. Then you dash back through the house, leading Nada to the window where you came in.

"It sounds like the entire household is after us," Nada comments as she swings out the window and into the tree. You follow, and as you jump down onto the wall, people are yelling at you from the window.

Go on to the next page.

"Which way?" Nada says. "They'll have every way out of the garden closed off."

"I know where we can go," you say. You jump down into the garden next door and take her to the lighted window you remember from earlier in the night. You knock on the partition, then open it and fall inside, where you find the man you followed engaged in deep conversation with his girlfriend.

Nada follows, and you quickly close the partition. You put your finger to your lips and say, "We won't stay long."

Turn to the next page.

82

For a tense half hour, you and Nada wait in silence. Outside, people shout, and torch lights flicker through the partition.

Finally, all is quiet again. You poke your head out the window and whisper, "I think they've moved on." You nod your thanks to the couple inside and begin climbing out. "Good luck," the man whispers to you.

You and Nada escape back through the garden and into the deserted western sector of the city, where Nada has a chance to tell you what happened.

"The idea was that Hitari and I would come into the past to find out exactly why his ancestor Mito was exiled. But we ran into you before we had a chance."

"Does that mean we still have to find out?" you ask.

"We can do that in a library—in the present," Nada says. "Right now, I want to get as far away from Hitari as I can."

The End

84

At daylight, you approach a gate to the city. The guards ask where you're from and who you're going to work for, which makes you a little more nervous about your disguise as a carpenter. But you answer with confidence and they let you in.

You walk down one of the wide avenues of the city, marveling at the mansions of the aristocracy. From behind you, voices order you to stand aside. You turn and watch an ornate ox-drawn carriage go plodding by, the nobleman inside scanning the passing scene. You try to stand out of the way, but he spots you. He orders one of his servants to bring you over to talk to him.

"Are you a carpenter?" he asks, eyeing your tools.

"Yes, my lord," you reply. Seizing a chance for information, you continue, "I am looking for the Hitari household. They want me to do a job for them."

"That's very good, but I need some repairs done on my mansion first. You'll come along with me." He closes his curtain before you can reply. His servants grab your sleeve, and you have no choice but to follow along behind the nobleman's carriage.

Turn to page 86.

86

At the lord's mansion, the house master has a long list of tasks for you. "First you can fix the roof. Then we want you to rebuild the wing where the second and third wives live, and then the pagoda in the garden." Seeing the look of dismay on your face, he says, "Don't worry. I'll give you three laborers to help. And you'll be well-paid for your work."

Go on to the next page.

You don't know what to do, except get to work on the roof and hope for a chance to make a getaway. You take your three helpers up to the roof but quickly realize you're in trouble. The men are waiting expectantly for your instructions, and you know next to nothing about the building techniques of the time.

Turn to the next page.

"Uh, I have to go get some more tools," you say as you back away from the three men squatting and eyeing you.

Just as you turn to leave, you step on a spot where the bark shingles have rotted through. They give way, and suddenly, you're falling. A noblewoman at her mirror screams as you plunge into her room. You start to get up, thinking only about escaping. But you quickly realize you won't be going anywhere—not with two broken legs.

The End

It's foolish to draw the sword when you don't really know how to use it, you decide, and besides, you might damage the tracking device. Keeping the sword sheathed, you slowly back up the trail. The two *ninja* advance, flanking you on either side.

"We told you to come alone!" one of them barks.

"I did," you respond. "Those men were reporters. They must have followed me. I didn't know they were here."

The *ninja* stop and one eyes you. "Are you Nada?"

"I'm her friend," you answer.

"That's the sword?"

"Yes."

"Put it down."

You set the sword on the ground. The *ninja* doing the talking comes forward to pick it up, while the other continues to advance on you, about to attack. Slowly you backpedal. When he gets closer, you pretend to lose your balance and start to fall backward. He rushes you. Your feet suddenly fly out, planting a two-footed kick in his chest and knocking him flat on his back. You spring up, leap over him, and race down the path.

You arrive panting back at the post office, where Nada and Detective Jonsuro are waiting.

"They got the sword," you gasp. "Where's Yoshi?"

"We haven't seen him yet," Jonsuro says. "But the tracking device is working."

Go on to the next page.

Detective Jonsuro takes you into the back of the post office where his men have set up a computer to follow the sword. You watch as they plot the course of the tracking device up the mountain. Near the top it abruptly stops. Jonsuro points to the map and says, "There's a temple right there. We'll give them twenty minutes to free Yoshi. Then we go after them."

The twenty minutes pass slowly. Yoshi does not appear, and the sword does not move. "Let's go!" the detective orders.

You and Nada follow Jonsuro and his officers back up the path. After a long climb, you finally reach the temple shown on the map. The police officers spread out for an assault on the temple. Jonsuro addresses the inhabitants through a megaphone, telling them they have two minutes to surrender. There's no answer.

Jonsuro motions to his officers, and they move in on the temple, their guns drawn. They kick in the front and back doors simultaneously and rush inside. A few minutes later, an officer reappears at the front door. "There's no one here," he announces.

You, Nada, and Jonsuro go into the temple. The sword has been driven into the floor. A note is stuck on the blade.

It is unfortunate for Yoshi, the note reads, that you chose to give me a fake. You were warned.

You wonder how you're going to explain this to Yoshi's parents.

The End

92

"I'm sorry, I can't teach you," you say to the *shugenja*. "The *sensei* who taught me pledged me to secrecy. I can tell you no more."

The *shugenja* seem disappointed, though they understand. "It is too bad," one says. "If you did choose to be a teacher, you would have many students. Nevertheless, you must be our guest at the monastery."

After you've shared a meal with the *shugenja*, you tell them you have to go to sleep. "I must get up before dawn," you say. "Can you tell me how to find the house of Mito Hitari?"

They consult among themselves before one of the monks says, "It is in the eastern sector, fourth ward, seventh block, where the second avenue meets the fifth cross street."

You repeat the instructions until you've got them memorized, thank the *shugenja* for their hospitality, and say good-night.

After a couple of hours of sleep, you're on your way back down the mountain to Kyoto. By the first rays of dawn, you're knocking on the door of the Hitari house. The *rojo,* or house mistress, sees your monk's clothes and asks politely what she can do for you. You decide to press your luck and ask if any visitors have arrived in the past day or two.

The *rojo* hesitates for a moment, then says, "Yes, a distant cousin of Lord Mito arrived yesterday."

"Could I see this cousin?" you say boldly.

The *rojo* is taken aback, but she says, "I'll find out. Wait a moment."

Go on to the next page.

The *rojo* returns and shows you in. "He asked that you wait for him back here," she says, leading you through the house to a small room in a far corner of the mansion.

The *rojo* leaves and you wait uncomfortably for the cousin to show up. As the wait goes on, you begin to suspect you're being set up. But then the *rojo* appears with a pot of tea, saying, "My lord apologizes for his lateness. He will be in to see you very soon."

You start sipping the tea, wondering if you should get out while you can. Then suddenly you stop drinking. The tea smells unusual, and you start to feel strange.

You've stepped into a trap, and there's only one way out. In an exaggerated motion, you stand up, wobble on your feet, and then collapse, breaking the teacup on the floor. You just hope you haven't already drunk enough poison that you will soon collapse altogether.

It takes only a few seconds for someone to appear. He drags you out of the room and down a corridor. You can tell by his strength that he must be a *ninja*. The only thing you have going for you is the element of surprise—as Nada has told you before, with it, you can defeat a much stronger enemy.

Turn to the next page.

You hear a sliding door open. The *ninja* grabs you, lifts you up underneath your arms, and takes you through the door in front of him, propping you up with his body. Suddenly, you feel cold steel against your neck, and he says with triumph, "I think things have changed now, Nada."

At the same moment that you hear Nada's sharp intake of breath, you stomp on the *ninja's* foot and simultaneously knock his knife arm back with your elbow.

He's caught completely off guard, and this gives Nada the opening she needs. She leaps and pins him to the floor with a single move. You work fast, tearing your monk's robes into strips and using them to tie up the *ninja*—but not fast enough. He screams for help.

The sound of footsteps comes from every direction. You look at Nada, silently asking, "Which way?"

Turn to the next page.

96

Nada points her finger in the air. She has two sets of *shuko*, or *ninja* claws, with her. You quickly put on one set. As you climb upward, you're pleased by how well the claws work on the wood of the walls. When you reach the top, you're amazed to see Nada punch a hole through the roof with her *shuko*. "I didn't know you could do that," you comment, as you follow her out of the hole.

Go on to the next page.

"Neither did I," she says.

You run along the top of the roof, leap into a tree, and climb down into the garden, from which you're able to escape into the city.

You lead Nada up the mountain toward the monastery. There you think you'll be able to find a safe place for the rituals required to return you and Nada to the present. On the way, you tell Nada how her grandmother helped you to come into the past and ask her if she's figured out what the *ninja* really wanted.

"As you know," she answers, "he wanted the sword. I came into the past because I didn't have any choice, but also because I wanted to find out if his ancestor Mito really had been wrongly exiled. I hadn't found that out yet when you arrived, but if Mito acted anything like the *ninja* did, I'm sure he deserved what he got."

The End

98

You leap into the driver's seat, put the car in gear, and take off. The taxi driver's yells fade behind you as you accelerate. But the trunk is shaking madly back and forth. The movement is rocking the car, and you can't keep a grip on the steering wheel. As you screech around a bend, you lose control. The car rolls, flipping over once and landing upright again.

You look out your window just in time to see the trunk, having broken loose from the roof, tumble over the edge of the road and down the mountain ravine.

You're bruised and bleeding, but you manage to drive the rest of the way to Nada's grandmother's house. "What happened?" Nada cries when you stumble in the door.

You tell her, finishing with the sight of the trunk careening down the ravine. "I don't see how he could have survived," you say, still a little in shock.

"The important thing is to take care of you," Nada says. She makes you lie down and dresses your wounds.

"What about your grandmother?" you ask, noticing a sleeping figure in the next room. "How is she?"

"She'll pull through," Nada says. "It's strange, though. I think it was a *ninja* poison that was making her sick. Luckily, I knew the antidote."

Turn to page 100.

100

You rest for a little while, but then you remember the car. "I've got to go find the taxi driver," you call to Nada, hobbling toward the door.

"You've got to go to a hospital," Nada replies firmly. "But I'll take you. I'll be out to the car in a minute."

You open the door and step outside. Darkness has fallen. Looking idly into the dark woods, your eye picks up a shape moving in the trees. You go to have a closer look. Suddenly, with a sharp intake of breath, you see the *ninja*, battered and bloody, trudging up the hill toward you!

Go on to the next page.

The *ninja* sees you a moment after you see him. He lets out a bloodcurdling scream and rushes toward you. Your instincts take over. You roll at his feet, tripping him over the top of you. He springs back to his feet and jumps on you, and you both go rolling and wrestling down the hillside. You can feel that he's weak from the accident—but so are you.

You stop rolling just short of a rocky drop-off and separate. Getting shakily to your feet, you await his next attack. But he has disappeared. You look all around. There's no sign of him.

You crouch and wait, listening. For several minutes there's nothing but the sound of the woods. You decide that if you stay where you are, you'll be an easy target.

You have to move, but where? You could climb a tree. From there you'd have a better vantage point, and you'd also have gravity on your side if a chance came to attack the *ninja*.

On the other hand, your strength is gone. Maybe you should go back to the house for Nada. That may be just what he expects you to do, but you could take a roundabout route.

If you climb a tree to gain a better vantage point, turn to page 76.

If you start back toward the house, turn to page 108.

102

"We don't have the sword," you say. "It's gone."

"You're lying," the *ninja* replies flatly.

"Let me explain," you plead. "If you mean the sword that once belonged to Sanchiro Miyamotori, it was sent to us anonymously last year, and—"

"I know it was sent to you last year," he interrupts.

"Well, then, who sent it?"

There's a moment of hesitation before he answers, "My brother sent it. But it is rightfully mine."

"Why did your brother send it to us?"

"That is none of your concern!" the *ninja* bursts out. "I demand that you return the sword to me."

"Why do you say it is yours?" you insist. "Are you a Miyamotori?"

"Yes! No!" His voice quavers. "Give me back the sword!"

"The sword is gone," you say gently. "There's no way to get it back."

"I don't believe you."

"I'll tell you the whole story," you propose. "Let's meet and talk."

"No!" Detective Jonsuro blurts out behind you. "It's too dangerous!"

"Who's with you?" the *ninja* demands.

If you ignore Jonsuro and again propose a meeting, turn to page 59.

If you heed the detective's warning, turn to page 107.

You jump out of the taxi and grab the driver. "Listen to me," you say, fixing him with your eyes. "There's a *ninja* in that trunk, and if you don't get us to where we're headed as fast as you can, he'll kill both of us."

The driver can tell you're serious. The two of you get back into the taxi, and he puts the pedal to the floor. The trunk is shaking so violently you think it might cause the car to flip. But the driver is good, and he somehow manages to keep the taxi on the road, screeching around the mountain curves as fast as he can.

At last you reach the long dirt driveway leading to Nada's grandmother's house. But just as you pull in, something punches through the roof of the car. A hand armed with *shuko* tears at the air between you and the driver. The steel claws hook on to the driver's collar and shake him fiercely. As you open your door to jump out, the driver loses control of the car. It crashes into a tree. You're tossed out, hitting the ground with a roll.

Nada runs from the house as you pop back onto your feet. The *ninja's shuko*-covered hand continues to shake the driver. You get back into the car, grab the *ninja's* wrist, and twist it. Nada jumps onto the roof and pries open the trunk. Once you get the claws out of the driver's collar, you continue to hold on to the *ninja's* wrist, hoping it will give Nada a chance to knock him unconscious again. Finally, the *ninja's* wrist goes limp as Nada gives him a hard crack on the neck. "Help me drag him inside the house," she calls.

Turn to the next page.

104

Once you have the *ninja* laid out and tied up in the house, you come back out to look for the driver. But apparently he's decided he's had enough—both he and the taxi are gone.

Back inside, you ask Nada how her grandmother is.

"Well, it's interesting," she says. "She's recovering. But I figured out that she was being poisoned. Not only that, it was a *ninja* poison."

"But why?" you wonder. "Was it to draw you away from the *dojo*?"

"Yes," Nada says. "And it must have been the work of this guy we've got tied up here. Tomorrow we'll turn the tables on him and find out what this is all about. But for now, I think we all need some rest."

The next morning you meet Nada's grandmother, Maki. She appears to be feeling much better. "Shall we start?" she says briskly.

You watch with fascination as she mixes an herb drink. "This will prepare him for *saiminjutsu*," she explains. You know from what Nada has taught you that *saiminjutsu* is a form of *ninja* hypnotism.

Maki feeds the *ninja* the potion as he begins to regain consciousness. Soon his eyes become glazed. Maki's magical *kuji* hand signs then put him under hypnosis.

Go on to the next page.

"What were you doing at the *dojo*?" she asks.

"The sword," the *ninja* says dreamily. "The sword of the Miyamotori. My sword."

"The one that was sent to the *dojo* last year!" you exclaim.

"Why did you want the sword?" Maki prompts.

"Its power—we have waited a thousand years to start our own *ryu*, and avenge our family...."

"What happened to your family?"

"My ancestor was sent into exile. But with the sword, I will avenge him."

Maki draws you and Nada into another room. "I sense the presence of a *kami*, a spirit," she says, "but an evil one. It may even be the *kami* of this ancestor of his who was sent into exile. Where is the sword he's talking about?"

"We no longer have it," Nada says. "It was destroying the *dojo*."

Turn to the next page.

106

"Here is what we must do," Maki instructs. "I will tell him that the sword no longer exists. Then I'll try to exorcise the *kami*. But you will have to leave us alone for a while."

Several hours later, you and Nada return to the room to find the *ninja* asleep. Maki has untied him.

"He will wake up in a few hours," she says.

"How did it go?" you ask.

Maki tries to be modest, but her pride shows through. "The exorcism worked," she says, "and he also understands that the sword is gone. I found out that he is a descendant of Mito Hitari. A thousand years ago, Mito was sent into exile for trying to kill his brother, of whom he was jealous. As we know, the curse of envy is that your spirit remains envious long after you have gone."

"And that was the spirit that possessed him?" you ask.

"Yes," Maki says.

"Where does the sword come in?" Nada asks.

"The Hitari are a branch of the Miyamotori family," Maki answers. "When the *ninja* heard about the sword, he became convinced that it could be the keystone for his *ryu*. Through the *ryu*, he thought he could restore his family's honor. But now he understands that he can start the *ryu* without the sword, and that he must let the past be. He was apologetic about what he did to you and Nada."

"Well," you say with a smile, "I guess Nada and I can let the past be too."

The End

"I *can't* meet with you," you say, following Detective Jonsuro's warning.

"Of course you can't meet me," the *ninja* replies acidly. "You know that I will see through your lie. You have the sword, and I want it!"

The call is disconnected. You turn to Nada and Jonsuro. "What now? He's more convinced than ever that we have the sword."

"We'll give him a fake," the detective says, "unless we can catch him first. He'll call again, and when he does, tell him you'll give up the sword."

The *ninja* does call again, the next day. "This is your last chance," he says.

"All right," you say, trying to sound defeated. "You can have the sword."

He gives you the location of a mountain temple where you are to leave the sword. "If you do everything correctly," he concludes, "Yoshi will be waiting for you in the village post office." Jonsuro has a sword forged from the description you give him. The next day he drives you and Nada up to a village near the temple. You take the fake sword into the temple alone. No one appears to be there. You leave the sword, and return to the village, hoping to find Yoshi. He's not there. You wait all day with Nada and Jonsuro, but Yoshi never appears.

The next day, the *ninja* calls again. "I don't need fakes," the *ninja* says angrily.

You never hear from him—or Yoshi—again.

The End

108

It's best to try to get help from Nada, you think, as you climb the hill. You don't want to go straight to the house, so you traverse the hillside, circling around to the other side, before continuing up to the house. All the while your ears are pricked for any sound that might give away the *ninja's* presence. But he seems to be nowhere near.

You approach the top of the hill and see the welcome light from the house only thirty yards away. You start to call out to Nada, but then you do hear a sound—the crunch of tires on gravel. Suddenly, the taxicab comes barreling over the edge of the hill, right at you. You're frozen in surprise. The last thing you see is the grille of the car.

The End

"Hiding out is not such a good idea," you say to Nada. "We might miss something important if we leave."

"Okay," Nada sighs.

You spend the rest of the day fending off reporters, and finally, after everyone has left, you lock the door and try to get some sleep. Early the next morning, you're jarred from a fitful sleep by a loud ringing.

"Hello," you say wearily into the telephone. The static on the line tells you the call is international.

"Nada Kurayama?" the man on the other end inquires.

"She's asleep," you say. "Can I help you?" The man sounds guarded. "I've heard about the kidnapping case. I have some information that may be of assistance to you."

This wakes you up. "What is it?"

"I understand the kidnapper wants a certain sword, a sword that once belonged to the Miyamotori family."

"Go on," you urge.

"If that is correct, I know who the kidnapper is." You wait for the man to continue.

"And I know where he is."

"Where?" you ask, a little skeptical.

Turn to the next page.

110

"I will tell you on one condition: when he is arrested, give him this message from his brother— tell him, 'This is the revenge of Taro.' If you promise to do that, I will tell you exactly where to find him."

Figuring you have nothing to lose, you say, "All right."

"There is a mountain above the village of Kanayama. You will find a path leading to a small temple on the mountain, a mile above the village. A complex of secret rooms is under the temple. You can get into the rooms through a trapdoor hidden beneath the cryptomeria tree to the west of the temple. You'll find my brother there. Don't forget the message."

After putting down the phone, you wake up Nada and call Detective Jonsuro.

"It's probably a prank call," Jonsuro says tiredly, "but we'd better check it out, anyway."

Turn to page 112.

112

Four hours later, you and Nada are following Jonsuro and his officers up a mountain path above the village of Kanayama. The trail climbs steeply, then suddenly crests on a clearing, in the middle of which sits a small temple. Jonsuro's officers retreat back down the trail a little way while you and Nada look for the trapdoor.

"It's right where the caller said it would be," you report to Jonsuro when you return.

"Okay. Here's the plan," Jonsuro says. "My men will storm the place through the trapdoor. You, Nada, and I will cover the temple, in case anyone tries to escape that way."

You and Nada creep into the temple with Jonsuro and hide while you wait for the police team to attack. A sudden burst of fighting sounds comes from below. Then all is quiet.

You wait for movement from underneath the temple. Sure enough, a trapdoor opens in the floor. You prepare to spring—then you see Yoshi! "You're safe!" you cry, running to hug him.

"When I heard the sound of people coming in, I used my training to escape from the two men who were guarding me," he explains.

You take him out of the temple and start down the trail. A few minutes later Jonsuro catches up. "There were four of them down there," he says. "Every single one committed *seppuku*. I guess they saw they couldn't escape arrest."

"Well, we may never know what this has all been about," you say, "but we got Yoshi back, and that's good enough."

The End

114

Vowing to be extra cautious, you take your first step up the stairs. Slowly, making no sound, pausing at each stair to listen, you ascend, your eyes fixed on the darkness above for any sign of movement.

Halfway up the staircase, your foot comes down gently on one of the steps. You put your full weight on the step and hear a splintering sound. Suddenly, the board gives way, and your leg falls through. You grasp for something to hold on to, but the whole staircase collapses. You tumble down to the floor below, wood and mortar crashing on top of you.

When all the crashing is over, you find yourself unable to move, buried underneath a pile of beams and boards. Even if you manage to get free somehow, Yoshi and the *ninja* will be long gone.

The End

You have only studied *kendo* a little bit, and you recollect your training now. You use the sky-to-ground movement to draw the sword, and let out a bloodcurdling yell at the same time.

To your surprise, the *ninja* locks eyes with you and is terrified. The *ninja* runs screaming into the woods. At first you think your *kendo* scared the *ninja*, but then you realize the *ninja* fears the sword itself, reputed to have fantastic powers.

You're not sure what to do next, so you decide just to keep going. You continue up the trail, sword drawn, ready for attack from any side, your ears attuned to the slightest sounds.

Then a voice speaks to you, loud and clear, as if someone is right next to you. You recognize it as the voice on the phone—the voice of the *ninja*. "Give me the sword," he says, "and I will spare your life."

You look all around—in the trees, on the ground, everywhere—to see where he could be hiding. But your trained eyes find nothing.

"This is your last chance," the voice says. "If you want to live."

You stop, and stand very still, sword raised, attuning to *sakki*, the presence of the killer.

In a flash, you whip the sword around to your left and above your head in the spinning-sword movement. It slices a falling branch in half—a split second before the branch would have hit your head.

The voice laughs. "Very good," the *ninja* says. "I see the sword still has its power."

Turn to the next page.

116

You crouch and turn with the sword, wondering what will happen next. Out of the corner of your eye, you see a black shape hurtling toward you. It's a person! You swing the sword and cut the body cleanly in half, only to find it was a stuffed dummy.

You try to move, but your foot is pinned to the ground by a wire. Suddenly, the *ninja* springs up from a trapdoor covered in pine needles, laughing as you struggle to free your foot.

You hack at the wire, but every time you do, the *ninja* advances on you, and you have to keep him at bay with the sword. He pulls out a *shuriken*. Just as he whips it at you, your foot comes free, and you dive out of the way. You roll and spring to your feet, ready to take on the *ninja*.

You circle each other for what seems like hours, but neither of you can make a move on the other.

Finally, you say, "I can see how much you want the sword. I'll hand it over to you if you show me Yoshi is safe."

"Shall we trade at the same time?" the *ninja* asks.

"Right," you say.

He nods once, and motions for you to follow him. He leads you down a tiny footpath through the woods to a shack disguised in leaves and branches. The *ninja* calls to someone inside to bring out Yoshi.

Yoshi's face lights up when he sees you. "Are you all right?" you ask him.

"I'm okay," he says a little shakily.

Turn to page 118.

118

You put the sword on the ground and slowly let go of it, watching as the *ninja* motions to his man to let go of Yoshi.

"Run, Yoshi!" you cry.

Yoshi bolts into the woods, and leaving the sword, you follow him. As you do, you see the *ninja* jump greedily to the sword.

"They're not chasing us," Yoshi says, looking over his shoulder.

You push him to keep running. "They will be when they figure out the sword is a phony."

You and Yoshi have enough of a head start that you make it back to the village, where Nada and Detective Jonsuro are waiting for you in the post office. Nada hugs Yoshi. Jonsuro is tracking the homing device on a map and sends a detachment of police out after the *ninja*.

Later, Yoshi is able to fill you in on why he was kidnapped. "The *ninja* said his family is a branch of the family that originally owned the sword. About a thousand years ago, his ancestor was sent into exile. All these years, his part of the family hasn't been able to restore their honor, but he thought by getting the sword he could start a powerful *ninja ryu*, a training school of his own. I guess he was going to use the school to get revenge."

"Well," Nada says, "that sword won't get him very far."

Although Jonsuro's men don't find the *ninja*, they do find the sword in the woods. Did the *ninja* discover it was a fake? You never know, because you never hear from the *ninja* again.

The End

"I'm staying here," you insist. "I can't abandon you."

The *shugenja* protest your decision. But soon there's no time for arguing as the first of the imperial regiment arrives. You hear yells and the clash of metal on metal. The guards are trying to push into the monastery. You rush to the door with the other *shugenja* in time to hear the regiment captain saying, "We only want the newcomer. There is no need to fight!"

People are running everywhere as the guards break through to the inside. There is hand-to-hand fighting all around you. You use kicks and punches to flatten several surprised guards. But more and more come pouring in, and finally, there are too many for you to handle. They pin you down and drag you outside. Some of the *shugenja* chase after, trying to free you, but the guards are too strong for them.

As you're shackled and taken back toward Kyoto, you smell smoke. You look back to see the monastery in flames.

You're quickly brought to trial at the Imperial Court and condemned to life in prison. Because of your legendary powers, you're under heavy guard twenty-four hours a day. Escape will be next to impossible. But you have a lifetime to try.

The End

You back out of the house slowly and soundlessly, wary now of traps that may be waiting for you. Outside, you circle around and find a vine growing up the back wall. You shimmy up the vine to a second-floor window and pull yourself inside.

You crouch beneath the window and listen. There are no sounds. Slowly and carefully you begin to investigate. In one of the rooms you find signs that the dust has been disturbed. Looking closer, you can make out fresh footprints.

Just then, you hear a muffled cry from downstairs, followed by running steps. You start for the stairs, but think better of it and return to the window you climbed in through. You hoist yourself back out, and as you begin to slide down the vine, a figure turns the corner below you.

Without hesitation, you leap, pushing off from the side of the house. In midair, you realize you're about to hit Yoshi, for the *ninja* is carrying him over his shoulders! You twist, trying to soften the impact, and hit a glancing blow with your feet off the *ninja's* thigh. He tumbles to the ground, and Yoshi flips over the *ninja's* head.

The *ninja* bounces back to his feet. Yoshi lies motionless on the ground. You and the *ninja* eye each other for a moment, then you spring at him. He flees into the brush. You start to give chase, but quickly turn back to see if Yoshi is all right.

Turn to the next page.

122

Yoshi is hardly breathing. You pat his cheek, trying to bring him to consciousness. Slowly he comes around. He looks at you foggily, barely recognizing you. You think the *ninja* must have poisoned him.

When Yoshi is able to respond to your questions, you check to make sure no bones are broken. You help him to his feet, but he sways woozily, and you notice an abrasion on the side of his head. Whether his wooziness is from having been drugged or from a possible concussion, you realize he won't be able to walk by himself.

You don't want to let the *ninja* go, but you have no choice. You must get Yoshi to a hospital. Perhaps later you'll have a chance to unravel the reasons behind Yoshi's kidnapping and track down the *ninja*. But right now, a long, hard night trip back to the *dojo* lies ahead of you.

The End

You want to use all your senses to deal with the intruder, so you don't use the earplugs.

Soon, you're hearing sounds from all over the house. First there's knocking at the front door, then pounding on the roof, then noises from the back. The sounds increase in volume and intensity until the whole building is shaking wildly. It seems as if the house is going to come apart.

The sounds are driving you mad. Finally, you realize you must get out of the house and escape the noise. You make a dash for one of the entrances to a network of secret passageways, where at least you'll be protected from a sneak attack.

But as you head for the secret door, you catch sight of a blur coming at you. Your reflexes are slow. Suddenly you're in the viselike grip of a *ninja*. Now you'll never have a chance to find out what this is all about.

The End

GLOSSARY

Aikido – Ai: "harmony"; ki: "energy"; do: "the way." A defensive practice using pivoting motions and the momentum of the attacker to neutralize an attack.

Dojo – The place where martial arts are practiced.

Furoshiki – A large kerchief used to tie up and carry one's belongings.

Hanbo – *Ninja* staff or stick.

Kaginawa – A grapple or hook attached to the end of a rope.

Kami – A spirit, demon, or deity.

Kendo – The art of sword fighting.

Kimono – A robe-like garment, usually cotton or silk, worn by men and women.

Kuji – *Ninja* sorcery. Sometimes described as "nine hands cutting" or "nine syllables." Mystic finger positions channel energy.

Kyoketsu shoge – A rope with a steel ring on the end.

Metsubishi – *Ninja* blinding powder, used to temporarily cloud the vision of an opponent.

Mikkyo – Esoteric knowledge, which is the highest knowledge of all.

Ninja – A person adept at the art of *ninjutsu*.

Ninjutsu – The "art of stealth" or "way of invisibility." An unconventional discipline incorporating martial arts, special weapons, techniques of concealment, and sorcery.

Obasa – Honorary title for a grandmother.

Onshinjutsu – Specific techniques of *ninja* invisibility.

Rojo – House mistress, woman in charge of the domestic staff.

Ryu – School or tradition of martial arts.

Saiminjutsu – *Ninja* hypnotism.

Sakki – A kind of sixth sense or ability to detect harmful intentions—"the force of the killer."

Samurai – Japanese feudal warrior. The *samurai* were the highest class, followed by farmers, craftsmen, and finally merchants. *Samurai* were also the administrators of the state.

Sensei – Master, teacher.

Seppuku – Ritual suicide, an honorable form of death for *samurai*.

Shugendo – A Japanese mountain religion incorporating ascetic practices and magic.

Shugenja – Mountain warrior priests or monks, practitioners of *Shugendo*. Similar to *Yamabushi*. Some aspects of *ninjutsu* developed out of their beliefs.

Shuko – Steel claws worn on the hands or feet.

Shuriken – A metal throwing blade, often star shaped.

Tengu – Mythical creatures supposed to have first taught *ninja* their art. Sometimes portrayed as helpful but mischievous, other times as devilish, *tengu* are often shown with long noses or beaks, wings attached to the body of an old man, and long claws or fingernails. They wear capes of feathers or leaves, live in trees in the mountains, and, according to one description, are the condensed spirit of the principle of *yin*, or darkness.

Yamabushi – Literally, "one who lies down on the mountains." A *Shugendo* priest, ascetic, or magician.

Yin and Yang – The polar forces of the universe, complementary opposites, whose alternation drives the processes of life.

ABOUT THE ARTISTS

Illustrator: Michael Tonn is an illustrator living in Burlington, Vermont. He has been interested in art for as long as he can remember. Many of his earliest memories are of his feverish attempts at putting down on paper the many characters inhabiting his imagination. Largely self-taught, Michael received his first professional experience illustrating for a local paper. In the rigors of the editorial illustration world, Michael learned many of the ins and outs of the craft. What started as a hobby, eventually blossomed into a full-time career, creating work for a wide variety of clients both nationally and internationally. Drawing inspiration from a variety of artists and periods, his style combines elements from classic illustration and cartooning with the exciting new possibilities of the digital age.

Cover Artist: Chloe Niclas has had a passion for drawing and visual narratives since she was four and, from a young age, knew it would be her life's work. She grew up in Baltimore, Maryland, and graduated from the Baltimore School for the Arts high school with a major in Visual Arts. She received her BFA in illustration from the Cleveland Institute of Art and went on to work at American Greetings, building comprehensive prototypes for new product concepts. Currently, she is transitioning into full-time freelance illustration work.

ABOUT THE AUTHOR

JAY LEIBOLD was born in Denver, Colorado. Jay has written *Secret of the Ninja, Sabotage, Grand Canyon Odyssey, Spy For George Washington, Return of the Ninja, The Search for Aladdin's Lamp, You are a Millionaire, Beyond the Great Wall, Revenge of the Russian Ghost, Surf Monkeys,* and *Ninja Cyborg* in the *Choose Your Own Adventure®* series.

For games, activities, and other fun stuff, or to write to Chooseco, visit us online at CYOA.com

The History of Gamebooks

Although the *Choose Your Own Adventure* series, first published in 1976, may be the best known example of gamebooks, it was not the first.

In 1941, the legendary Argentine writer Jorge  Luis Borges published *Examen de la obra de Herbert Quain* or *An Examination of the Work of Herbert Quain,* a short story that contained three parts and nine endings. He followed that with his better known work, *El jardín de senderos que se bifurcan,* or *The Garden of Forking Paths,* a novel about a writer lost in a garden

Jorge Luis Borges maze that had multiple story lines and endings.

More than 20 years later, in 1964, another famous Argentine writer, Julio Cortázar, published a novel called *Rayuela* or *Hopscotch.* This book was composed of 155 "chapters" and the reader could make  their way through a number

Julio Cortázar

of different "novels" depending on choices they made. At the same time, French author Raymond Queneau wrote an interactive story entitled *Un conte à votre façon,* or *A Story As You Like It.*

Early in the 1970s, a popular series for children called *Trackers* was published in the UK that contained multiple choices and endings. In 1976,

Journey Under the Sea, 1st Edition

R. A. Montgomery wrote and published the first gamebook for young adults: *Journey Under the Sea* under the series name *The Adventures of You*. This was changed to *Choose Your Own Adventure* by Bantam Books when they published this and five others to launch the series in 1979. The success of CYOA spawned many imitators and the term gamebooks came into use to refer to any books that utilized the second person "you" to tell a story using multiple choices and endings.

Montgomery said in an interview in 2013: "This wasn't traditional literature. The *New York Times* children's book reviewer called *Choose Your Own Adventure* a literary movement. Indeed it was. The most important thing for me has always been to get kids reading. It's not the format, it's not even the writing. The reading happened because kids were in the driver's seat. They were the mountain climber, they were the doctor, they were the deep-sea explorer. They made choices, and so they read. There were people who expressed the feeling that nonlinear literature wasn't 'normal.' But interactive books have a long history, going back 70 years."

Young R. A. Montgomery

Choose Your Own Adventure Timeline

1977 – R. A. Montgomery writes *Journey Under the Sea* under the pen name Robert Mountain. It is published by Vermont Crossroads Press along with the title *Sugar Cane Island* under the series name *The Adventures of You*.

1979 – Montgomery brings his book series to New York where it is rejected by 14 publishers before being purchased by Bantam Books for the brand new children's division. The new series is renamed *Choose Your Own Adventure*.

1980 – *Space and Beyond* initial sales are slow until Bantam seeds libraries across the U. S. with 100,000 free copies.

1983 – CYOA sales reach ten million units of the first 14 titles.

1984 – For a six week period, 9 spots of the top 15 books on the Waldenbooks Children's Bestsellers list belong to CYOA. *Choose* dominates the list throughout the 1980s.

1989 – Ten years after its original publication, over 150 CYOA titles have been published.

1990 – R. A. Montgomery publishes the *TRIO* series with Bantam, a six-book

series that draws inspiration from future worlds in CYOA titles *Escape* and *Beyond Escape*.

1992 – ABC TV adapts Shannon Gilligan's CYOA title *The Case of the Silk King* as a made-for-TV movie. It is set in Thailand and stars Pat Morita, Soleil Moon Frye and Chad Allen.

1995 – A horror trend emerges in the children's book market, and Bantam launches *Choose Your Own Nightmare*, a series of shorter CYOA titles focused on creepy themes. The subseries is translated into several languages and converted to DVD and computer games.

1998 – Bantam licenses property from *Star Wars* to release *Choose Your Own Star Wars Adventures*. The 3-book series features traditional CYOA elements to place the reader in each of the existing *Star Wars* films and feature holograms on the covers.

2003 – With the series virtually out of print, the copyright licenses and the *Choose Your Own Adventure* trademark revert to R. A. Montgomery. He forms Chooseco LLC with Shannon Gilligan.

2005 – *Choose Your Own Adventure* is re-launched into the education market, with all new art and covers. Texts have been updated to reflect changes to technology and discoveries in archaeology and science.

2006 – Chooseco LLC, operating out of a renovated farmhouse in Waitsfield, Vermont, publishes the series for the North American retail market, shipping 900,000 copies in its first six months.

2008 – Chooseco publishes CYOA *The Golden Path*, a three volume epic for readers 10+, written by Anson Montgomery.

2008 – Poptropica and Chooseco partner to develop the first branded Poptropica island, "Nabooti Island" based on CYOA #4, *The Lost Jewels of Nabooti.*

2009 – *Choose Your Own Adventure* celebrates 30 years in print and releases two titles in partnership with WADA, the World Anti-Doping Agency, to emphasize fairness in sport.

2010 – Chooseco launches a new look for the classic books using special neon ink.

2013 – Chooseco launches eBooks on Kindle and in the iBookstore with trackable maps and other bonus features. The project is briefly hung up when Apple

has to rewrite its terms and conditions for publishers to create space for this innovative eBook type.

2014 – Brazil and Korea license publishing rights to the series. 20 foreign publishers currently distribute the series worldwide.

2014 – Beloved series founder R. A. Montgomery dies at age 78. He finishes his final book in the *Choose Your Own Adventure* series only weeks before.

2018 – Z-Man Games releases the first-ever Choose Your Own Adventure board game, adapted from *House of Danger*. Record sales lead to the creation of a new game for 2019 based on *War with the Evil Power Master.*

2019 – Chooseco publishes a new sub-series of Choose Your Own Adventure books based on real-life spies. The first two of the series are *Spies: Mata Hari* and *Spies: James Armistead Lafayette,* by debut authors Katherine Factor and Kyandreia Jones.

2019 – The first-ever *Choose Your Own Adventure* audiobooks are released, with voice-activated interactive technology. These audiobooks include *Journey Under the Sea, The Abominable Snowman, The Magic of the Unicorn,* and more.

CHOOSE YOUR OWN ADVENTURE®

SPIES:
MATA HARI

BASED ON A TRUE STORY

BY KATHERINE FACTOR